THE UNKNOWN MAN

Tales from the Sidelines of Corporate Jungles and Social Life at Different Geographies

RADHA KONDA

Dedication

*To all the gorgeous personalities who crossed my
path in my corporate and social life.*

Contents

Foreword

*T*he *Unknown Man* is a random collection of short stories that a creative mind has moulded and assimilated over decades. It has the elements of life as closely seen as possible. It has narration that delves into fine details and the depth of human mind. It has experience that transcends boundaries.

It has learning from the simple instances in life that teaches; only if you are a keen listener. It is as much about life-changing scary dreams as it is about meeting the unknown man, who is the absolute love! It is about nascent adolescent escapades and surmounting language barriers. It is about life's adventures and of finding ways to turn one's shortcomings into a positive campaign. You will find all this and more in *The Unknown Man*.

I am sure reading through this rather small volume, you will be tempted to revisit instances in your own life, its joys and hardships, its teachings and also recall the unknown men who helped you in your journey. When that happens, it would be the best experience of *The Unknown Man* that you will love to have!

The author, K S Radhakrishnan, aka Radha Konda, is a prolific writer in Tamil and English and has woven Blog spots of his experiences. A keen observer of human behaviour, he brings to life the depth of the human mind through the simple settings and behaviours in his stories. A process optimisation professional in the manufacturing sector to start with, he has doubled up as a Customer Experience and Strategy Adviser to the Banking Sector and as an adjudicator of Corporate Business Excellence and Quality awards. With a special love for creative graphic designs that speaks for itself, his innovative pursuits include writing punch-filled limericks almost daily.

Without hesitation, pick your copy and read it in one go. You will love it.

R. Easwaran

A Retired Senior Official from
Bharat Heavy Electricals Limited,
Tiruchirappalli, India

Preface

This is a collection of alluring tales on the sidelines of my corporate and social life. The incredible range of personalities that I came across and the exciting anecdotes at exotic locations far and wide were the backdrop to conjure my thoughts. Surely, there was a side-story at every turn in the corporate and social life. I strongly feel those are the tales that are worth telling.

These accounts allude to bundles of emotions; like, unexpected acts of kindness, unadulterated adolescent escapades, fun and frolic, self-pity at lack of deftness at times, my hits, and misses, and plenty of other sentiments rolled into separate stories.

By packing all these anecdotes in *The Unknown Man*, what I have attempted is to relive these emotions all at once. I am putting them forward to you, with the confidence that you will enjoy reading them, feel entertained and worth your time.

Here are some notes about the anecdotes. A few of my acquaintances have indicated to me that they would like to stay anonymous. Respecting such calls for privacy, I have laid these accounts on a camouflaged canvas, using pseudonyms. All characters and situations are fictionalised and do not refer to any person living or dead or any event - although they take inspirations from real-life personality traits and anecdotes. There may be some stretching of facts, only to make them more impactful – taking a kind of poetic liberty.

Let us not wait any further in welcoming *The Unknown Man.*

Radha Konda

(K S Radhakrishnan)

Acknowledgement

I thank my friend Shri R Easwaran for taking the time to read the manuscript, suggest valuable edits, and for presenting a Foreword for this book.

I am grateful to Shri Bibek Debroy and Shri Arun Krishnan for reading the book and writing blurbs for it.

CHAPTER ONE

The Incomplete Death 'Sentence'

"Rajesh, I am now going to declare your date of expiry. Listen carefully. Your date of expiry is...." a commanding and intimidating voice thundered from nowhere.

Rajesh gasped heavily and sweated profusely. He pleaded with all humility. Brushing aside all his pleadings, the voice continued the pronouncement.

"... twenty-seventh of May, two thousand ..." the voice said.

Rajesh woke up with a shock. Found himself sitting in the living room of his apartment.

On working days, Rajesh Kumar usually gets up at around 6:30 a.m. But today was different. He had disturbed sleep and woke up too early, at around 4 a.m. After coming out of the bedroom, he sat on a couch in the living room and stretched himself.

'Maybe after a while, I would have slept off in a sitting posture on the couch,' he thought.

'Was the pronouncement a dream?' he asked himself.

Normally, dreams for Rajesh would be hazy like soft clouds here, there, and everywhere, and he would be floating on them. They would be disjointed. They would lack firmness, clarity, and sharpness. But this morning's assertion about his expiry date was very concrete, loud, and clear. Rajesh found it hard to brush it aside as a dream.

'Is it then for real?' The thought that it appeared so made him more nervous.

Wait. The date mentioned was 27th May, but he could not recollect the year. As the pronouncement was going on, did he wake up or regain consciousness too soon and miss out on the year?

All his efforts to recall the year didn't bear fruits. He was hoping that during the course of the day, he would find the year-answer.

But Rajesh's restlessness and fear grew as time passed.

Let us know more about Rajesh Kumar. After his B.Sc. Maths graduation, Rajesh targeted a bank job, that too with public sector banks. After several attempts, he succeeded in getting one with a public sector bank.

At his office, he stuck to the boundary lines of his job, not because of his love for job descriptions – but he hated doing anything extra, even if that would help his team or bank.

In addition, he would always nitpick on the input papers he received from other departments or his own team members.

He would ring-fence himself from any additional tasks. He sported an irritable face that kept people seeking help away, in turn preventing additional tasks that might come by.

Simply, he followed the 'leave me alone' principle. Obviously, he had only a few friends in the office and he was nicknamed 'touch me not.'

At home, too, he was not an easy to approach husband or dad. When Rajesh's nickname reached their home, after many touch points, his wife Padma and their only son Siddharth, Sidhu in short, weren't surprised. They, in fact, had the reinforcement that Rajesh is the same in office, at home and everywhere.

When dealing with him, over the years, Padma mellowed to generally maintain a quiet demeanour. But Sidhu took more liberty in pulling his dad's legs, which would naturally result in some showdowns at home. After Sidhu moved to the US to pursue his MS degree, the distance reduced such encounters gradually.

The pronounced date of expiry kept flashing in Rajesh's mind. He was still unable to recollect the year. But when he saw the day's date, he was stunned.

'Oh! Today is 28th May 2021. How did I miss it?' he cursed himself.

'27th May, was the date of expiry pronounced.'

'27 May 2021 is over. So, the earliest year is 2022. I have one year more at least!' he worked out.

The tasks he had to complete before his death quickly flashed in his mind. He became more worried.

'Should get Sidhu married,'

'Should make a list of things to do,'

He recollected the life insurance policy he had taken when he joined the bank 26 years ago. It was for some eight lakh rupees. It appears to be a pittance now. 'Need to check if I can increase the policy amount now,'

'All bank accounts and FDs are in joint holding with Padma. No issues there,'

'Have invested in some mutual funds. I need to check if all of them have a nominee added,'

'Need to make arrangements for Sidhu's tuition fees for the next year,'

'Immovable properties are this apartment and an old house in the native place,'

'Should I write a will to ensure clarity?'

He kept getting random thoughts. He wondered from whom he can take advice – being a lone ranger all his life, none flashed in his mind, which triggered another series of thoughts of philosophical nature.

'What have I achieved in my life?'

'What is the legacy I am leaving behind?'

'Will people around miss me?'

'Or will they feel relieved with my absence?' This particular reflection sunk him in depression.

Padma was coming out from the kitchen to give Rajesh his early morning coffee.

Rajesh decided, 'Let me not show any nervousness. I should stay normal.'

He sipped the coffee given to him.

"Coffee tastes good," he said with calmness.

Padma was pleasantly surprised as she is used to comments like:

'Coffee is not hot enough,'

'Less decoction,'

'Sugar is not enough,'

'Milk is overheated.'

Padma wondered, 'What happened to him today?' and gave him an inquisitive stare.

After his morning coffee, as usual, Rajesh went about watering the plants in the balcony across the living room. These pots were placed in the balcony when he bought this apartment few years ago. He used to love watering of plants, but over the years it gradually became a chore to him.

But today, when he watered them, he felt like giving life to life. He lovingly caressed the leaves and cleaned the dirt on them.

He dusted the books and bookshelf in the living room and placed the books in order. He was aware that he was doing this after a long, long time.

Padma, who came to the living room to collect the coffee cup, noticed his behaviour. She continued to observe him throughout the day.

After taking bath, Rajesh went to the pooja room for prayers. Today, he felt like lighting the ceremonial lamp. He put the wick and added oil. Looked around for the matchbox; couldn't find it.

"Padma, where is the matchbox?"

Padma wondered why he was interested in lighting the lamp today. It was too unusual.

"It is in the second drawer, on the right side," she told him the precise location of the matchbox. She is known for her orderliness.

Rajesh lit the lamp and completed his prayers. He did pray for a while, a time longer than usual.

Padma surely continued to take note of his unusual behaviour today.

As Rajesh sat down at the dining table for breakfast, Padma hesitantly said, "The dosa batter I prepared hasn't been fermented yet. So, I have cooked upma, or do you want oats porridge?"

Rajesh, who generally likes to take idli or dosa for breakfast, replied softly, "It is fine, I'll have upma."

For Padma, who is used to abrasive retorts from Rajesh, his reply gave her some new, unfamiliar pleasantness.

Maybe driven by some guilt, she asked him, "Can I fry some fish for lunch? I have kingfish in the fridge."

"No. No non-veg, today.." he murmured.

Padma wasn't sure if he meant 'today' or 'from today.' Acknowledging that Rajesh was in deep contemplation, she decided to wait for an appropriate time to clarify this point with him. She intensified her observation of Rajesh.

In the meantime, Rajesh was digging deep into his mind for the year-answer. But was still unsuccessful.

During these COVID-inflicted lockdown days, Rajesh worked from home.

Upon joining the bank, Rajesh started with a posting in the Chennai Chepauk branch. Then, he moved to branches in Tiruvannamalai and Tumkur and finally to Nagpur. After serving in four branches, he moved to the bank's centralised back office in Chennai. In fact, his key criteria for moving to the back office was to keep away from 'customer-interaction-troubles'!

He is now a Project Manager in the Projects department. He has to follow up on the status of the projects with various stakeholders and report to the

Head of Projects. The company's laptop and mobile phone, as well as remote meetings through MS Team, are his tools and wherewithal.

Since Rajesh started working from home, Padma had noticed him raising his voice often and quickly getting into arguments. She was aware that this was his personality trait but was expecting that he would be a little more refined in office dealings. It was not to be.

But today, it has been totally different. She was surprised to see Rajesh talking to his colleagues softly and closing the conversations pleasantly. She could observe that his behaviour has had a total transformation.

'What happened to Rajesh?' she wondered. She decided to update Sidhu on this turn-around on that night's call with him. Normally, she speaks to Sidhu at around 8:30 p.m. India time, as this is a convenient time for Sidhu in the US.

Padma waited for dinner to be over while Rajesh was still struggling to recollect the 'answer' to the year question.

At the stroke of 8:30 p.m., she called Sidhu from the bedroom.

"Hi, mom, how are you?"

"Fine Sidhu. Had your breakfast?" Padma opened with a typical affectionate mom question.

"Just now I got up. Will eat after some time. Tell me. Second dose of vaccine is due for you both. When is your appointment?"

"Next Thursday. But there is something more important I have to tell you. Listen carefully....." She went on to explain in detail to her son Rajesh's changed behaviour today, from early morning...appreciative of morning coffee, eating upma, watering plants with care, breakfast conversation, and the poise with which he attended his office duties.

In the meantime, Rajesh, who was in the living room, also wanted to talk to his son Sidhu.

He started to move towards the bedroom, uttering, "Padma, are you talking to Sidhu? Hold on. I also want to speak to him."

As Padma was engrossed in explaining the 'bizarre' developments at home to Sidhu, she neither heard Rajesh nor realised that he had already reached the doorstep of the bedroom and was hearing her last bit of conversation with Sidhu.

That was the moment Padma was making an important concluding statement on Rajesh, "Sidhu.. looking at your dad's behaviour today, I can say that his old avatar is dead, and today we have a new avatar born!"

Rajesh was stunned by this 'answer.'

CHAPTER TWO

"Don't Rubbish Your Rubbish"

"Sh...How many heads will roll this year?" and "Who will get the pink slip?" were the questions flashing in my mind as my boss stepped out of his office to attend the crucial management committee meeting.

I am Ramnath, I work in a multinational company in Dubai. Before knowing about me and my job, it would be good to know about my boss.

He is David Hull, a Britisher. He is our Chief Financial Officer, and is a part of the most powerful trio of our company. The other two are the Chief Executive Officer and Chief Business Officer.

This trio calls all the shots in the company. David Hull being the trigger for all such shots, and he propels them with analysis and data. Amongst the trio, employees fear David the most, for his ruthlessness in making demands. Working with him is like sitting on the edge of a sword. Amongst the employees, he is also known as the 'slayer'! Apart from the Finance function, David Hull takes care of strategic planning too.

My duty, as a qualified MBA Finance, is to assist David in preparing performance reports, strategic plans and following up their implementation. In short, I am the Executive Assistant to the CFO. With such a boss, my working hours are always stretched.

Let's travel back to last week.

That day, it was past 7 p.m., and I was still in my office preparing some reports. Everyone else had left for the day except for some Office Boys who were cleaning the office.

The most important management committee meeting of the year has been scheduled for next week. The performance of the company and all functions will be reviewed. I expect a lot of red flags, which will lead to cost-cutting measures like layoffs. Everyone will be keeping their fingers crossed to hold their jobs.

I finished all the reports and data requested by David and was weeding off the unwanted papers and dumping them in the dust bin.

"Sir, doing your month-end cleaning?"

I looked up.

It was Balan, the Office Boy who runs errands for CFO's functions. Balan is an interesting character. A bit garrulous, a kind of loud-mouthed, but intelligent. He has the habit of making comments beyond his level at office. He hails from Kerala, India.

I am fluent in Malayalam as I had my 5 years of schooling in Trivandrum, Kerala, where my father had his job posting during that period. He speaks to me in Malayalam. Balan used this Malayalam connection to take liberty with me. I tolerated him for two reasons.

One, you would have guessed - a fellow countryman speaking in Malayalam with me.

Second, while Balan is talkative, he is resourceful too in providing inside stories about employees and happenings in the company, in particular of Finance department.

Our CEO's office is on the ninth floor of our building. David is in the next office. His secretary sits next to his office close to the visitors' lounge. My office is located next to the lounge.

Finance department has seven employees. Haitham, the Financial Controller, heads the department. All of them occupy one corner of the eight floor. Balan serves as the Office Boy for them too. So, I get a direct relay of the happenings in that floor, through Balan.

As I continued to dump trash in the bin, I answered, "Yes" to Balan's query of "Sir, doing your month-end cleaning?"

"Sir. Wouldn't it not be easy to dump now and then rather than wait for a month?" Balan opened his loud mouth gently.

I was irritated at his comments, although I knew that he was making a sensible point.

Without answering him, I continued to sort and dispose the papers – confidential ones into the shredder and others into the waste bin under my table. In addition, my mind was preoccupied thinking about the crucial decisions that would come out of the next week's management committee meeting.

Balan may have sensed that I didn't like his nosy comment. He changed the topic and started talking about employees in the Finance department.

"Sir, the eighth floor Haitham, too, does large-scale cleaning at the end of the month like you. He is studious and always very busy at work. Never waste time in chatting with others. He is always immersed in work."

It is well-known that Egyptian Haitham is a star performer in the company. I did notice Balan's attempt to please me by comparing me with Haitham to salvage the situation.

"Is it?" I curtly replied.

"But Sir, you that Amir in Finance - the Lebanese peron. He vanishes from his seat very often. I think he goes out of the office without informing his boss, Haitham. He takes bank loans and splurges. He is a spendthrift. Buys fancy cars and changes them often. Now, it appears that he has defaulted on loans, and bank collectors are after him. They even visited our office to meet him to collect the defaulted amount. That's why he goes out frequently." He gave a pause and continued, "With all these, I don't know how he can work effectively in the office."

I was surprised. Since joining the company, Amir was considered to be a responsible person. Maybe there is a recent change in his life style now, I pondered.

"Oh!" I replied, trying to appear uninterested.

But there is no stopping Balan! Although he had finished his work, he stayed back to chat with me.

"But the others seated next to Amir, I mean Pakistani Rasheed, Sri Lankan Chanaka, our Gujarati Viyas, Bengali Banerjee are not like Amir. They are all busy at work. They take breaks only for lunch, coffee, and tea." That was Ramesh's commendation for these four Finance employees.

'Has Balan missed one count in the Finance department?' I wondered when Balan promptly continued.

"Sir, that Goa lady Stella is horrible. Always on the mobile phone! She keeps chatting with her husband, children, and friends in rotation. If she is not talking, she will be on WhatsApp! Or, munching some chocolates! She is a waste, Sir!" he completed with an assertion.

Without showing any expression, I gave an 'is-that-so' look.

Balan may have thought that I did not believe his observations, but he continued the conversation.

"Sir, do you need proof for what I said?" he continued unabated. "After everyone leaves the office in the evening, just look into their dustbin, Sir. The bins will reveal their character, Sir!"

I was taken aback and looked up at him with a little more seriousness now.

"Wow. This guy is bringing validations for his assessment," I was about to compliment him in wonderment.

"Sir, you and Haitham do monthly clean-up very regularly. Monthly cleaning is not a problem. You both dump papers in an orderly fashion."

"This makes it easy to collect trash. There is no need for daily change of the plastic bag of your bins." I remembered seeing the black plastic bag inserted into every dustbin.

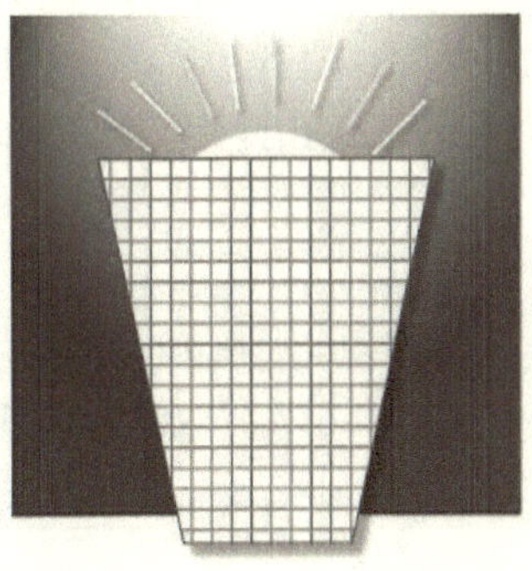

Balan continued.

"All are not like this, Sir. This Amir crumbles papers, maybe in frustration, and throws them in the bin. The bin will get full often. In addition, he dumps chewing gums that he munches all the day. This makes the bin sticky and messy when collecting the junk."

"Some people eat at the desk and dump all the leftovers in the bin under their desks, rather than disposing of them in the bin at the pantry. After a while, this leaves a stink if not cleaned quickly."

"It is difficult and messy to clean their bins. The plastic bags need to be changed often. Otherwise, it will leave a stink in the office."

"Not just in the Finance department. Such people are in all departments" Balan's outburst about people who lack discipline was unstoppable but very pertinent.

His conversation appeared to me as a presentation at a conference on cleanliness sans PowerPoint!

Under the watchful eyes of Balan, I gathered the last few papers for dumping and tore them in an orderly fashion. Then I resisted the usual temptation of throwing them in the bin, by carefully placed them in the bin. His observations have already put me in a deep thought.

"Sir, I have so much to tell like this. But you have already branded me as a loud-mouth!" he accused me with some liberty. After uttering these words, he moved away from my desk.

I contemplated, 'Like digital footprints, the junk footprints too can be a useful tool to analyse human psychology. Can we call it Balan's junkology? Wow!'

I collated all the reports and analysis David wanted. I double-checked and ensured if all are in order, and left the office for home.

While driving back home, I was ruminating on the company's status. The reports I prepared reveal that company's financials aren't that healthy. While costs are on the rise, sales and revenue have been stagnant. If these don't improve, then the company will have to get into cost-cutting and layoffs.

Such layoffs are not uncommon amongst MNCs, and they are also true with companies in Dubai. I myself have seen many layoffs in our own company, and the nervousness that creeps amongst employees, including me, is dreadful. The next management committee meeting is looming large in everyone's minds. Crucial decisions will come out, including layoffs. I am sure heads will roll in all departments, including Finance. The reports that I prepared will be reviewed by David and other senior managers days before this meeting.

The cost-cutting matter is primarily owned by David, who will reel out data to nail decisions. He is the data-king. All his proposals have the weight of data and statistics to support. He will come out with recommendations to bolster company's profitability - dispassionately, all backed by bullet-proof data. Weeks of preparation of reports will see their logical end at this meeting.

While David engages me in all the reports and recommendations, he will keep me away from the ones leading to cost-cutting and layoffs. Obviously, for the reasons of confidentiality.

Today is the day of the important management committee meeting! As I mentioned at the start, David just left his office to attend the management committee meeting. The conference room is in one corner of the ninth floor. I can see it from my office. The trio will be present throughout the meeting, and the department heads will be called in turns to attend, when their agenda comes up for discussion.

As scheduled, the meeting started at 10:00 a.m. and would be expected to last about 2 to 3 hours.

Time ticked like an impending bomb.

Around 12:20 p.m., the meeting got over and I could see David and Haitham coming out of the conference room and heading towards David's office.

As David walked into his office along with Haitham, he looked at me and said, "Ramnad, come in." That is how he calls me.

As soon as he sat down, he entrusted me with a folded slip and said, "Inform the HR Head to prepare termination letters for these two. Ask her to consult Haitham to finalise the letters."

I was too eager to open and look at the names. But I thought it would be unwise to open it when David was still speaking. Since it was handed over to me, I was relieved that my name is not there.

David asked Haitham, "Reduce one headcount in Finance and find a replacement for the other through internal vacancy. Work with HR."

So, two persons have lost their jobs in Finance. Across the company, it could easily be twenty-five people, I quickly guessed.

David looked at me and nodded that I could leave his office.

I rushed to my desk and opened the slip.

I was too eager to know the names of the two employees who were losing their jobs.

When I saw the names, my eyes widened.

The reason?

Hundreds of manhours and several management tools were used in preparing the detailed proposals, and decisions were taken by the management committee based on that.

This particular 'informed' decision preciously matched with the observations of our loud-mouth Balan!

CHAPTER THREE

What's in a Name?

After overcoming the terrible traffic jam in Guindy Road, Karthik reached Chennai domestic airport terminal, just in time. Wiping his sweat, he quickly checked in and walked into the waiting area after passing through the security check.

Today's official trip is to attend the urgently-called DXB project team meeting in Mumbai. As he was looking around for a seat at the gate, he saw a burly, balding gentleman already sitting there.

Karthik immediately recognised him. He is Rakesh Shukla, his batchmate at National Institute of Technology (NIT) Trichy. Rakesh, a Delhiite, whose patronage of the *dhaba* eateries outside NIT campus was legendary. Rakesh did Electronics and Communication, and Karthik, Production Engineering. Being the students from different disciplines, they have had little interactions. But they worked together for a few days as volunteers in the cultural committee of *Festember* event of NIT. Rakesh found it difficult to recollect Karthik's name.

"Hi, Rakesh," said Karthik as he shook his hand.

"Do you remember my name?" Karthik asked him with a queer in his voice. Karthik has always been particular, or can we say obsessed, about personalised approaches - he expected to be addressed by his name and practised what he believed in. He has the passion and ability to remember names. He addresses people by their names. In short, he is a name-fanatic.

Rakesh said, "Yes. No.." and with a now-I-found-you excitement, "Yes.. you were in room 16," to the embarrassment of Karthik. 16 was the hostel room number where Karthik stayed in the last 3 years of his under-graduation.

With his love for names, Karthik naturally gets upset when addressed as a 'number.' But in this fast-paced world, there is a growing trend of numbers replacing names in all walks of life, making our Karthik suffocate.

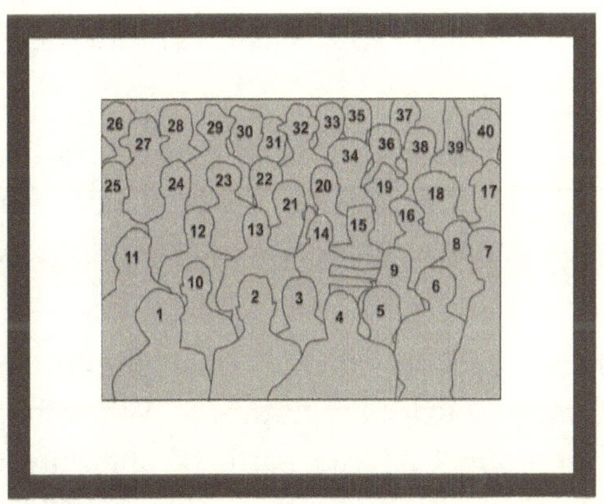

"Come on, Rakesh, I am Karthik." They exchanged their business cards and notes on the whereabouts of other classmates. After a while, Karthik left to board his flight to Mumbai.

On the flight, before setting the mobile on flight mode, Karthik added Rakesh's contact details to the mobile. A look at the number pad on the mobile reminded him of the name vs number battle. He used to think that life was all about making a name, but a closer look at the conversation with Rakesh and other daily events makes him wonder if one's name matters at all anymore. As he stretched himself in his seat, he recollected the previous day's incidents.

Karthik's credit card stopped working and he had applied for a replacement card. Considering his frequent official travels, he preferred to collect it from his branch. At his turn, he approached the counter. Reading the staff's name from the nameplate displayed, he said "Mr. Nagaraj. I am Karthik. I want to collect my credit card."

"Sir, can I have your customer number or card number?"

Karthik wondered if his name was not good enough. Maybe sensing this, the staff said, "Customer number or card number will make things easy and quick, Sir."

Karthik reached to his smartphone and said, "536719 is my customer number." When he left the bank after collecting the card, disappointment was writ on his face that '536719' is more valuable than his name in this set up.

Around 6:00 p.m. on the same day, Karthik walked into Aster clinic for his hypertension. Receiving his waiting token number from the attendant, which was

23, Karthik asked, "Mr. Sundar, when will I get my turn?"

"Sir, now number 17 is in. It might take at least 45 minutes for you," said the attendant, a bit surprised at being addressed by his name. After a while, there was a shout from the attendant:

"Who is 23?" and recognising Karthik, he said, "Sir, you are twenty-three. It is your turn. Go in."

After the consultation, Karthik walked out of the doctor's cabin to the now familiar voice of Sundar, shouting, "Who is 24?"

Karthik's hypertension had another cause to worry, as he realised that here again, the number won the battle over the name.

Upon landing in Mumbai, Karthik checked into his hotel and called his wife.

His wife said, "Karthik, don't forget to collect my sari from Asok." Asok is Hema's brother living in Mumbai.

"But, Hema, I am taking a return flight tonight; it is not possible to meet Asok."

"Okay. I will ask him to pass it on to the hotel reception," said Hema.

Karthik reminded, "Hema, make a note, Hotel Residency, Andheri. Room 505. Ask Asok to write my name on the parcel."

Middle of the day, there was a WhatsApp message in his mobile: 'Medicine given to hotel. Hema.'

The meeting took longer than expected, and only a couple of hours were left before Karthik's return flight. After the meeting, noting that he couldn't waste any time, Karthik didn't wait to chat with anyone and rushed to the hotel.

At the reception, ahead of him, there was another gentleman, "I am Hemant Ghosh. Do I have any message?" he asked.

"Can I have your room number, Sir" he heard the staff at the reception ask that gentleman. Karthik realised that there is no stopping of this number-rampage. Time was ticking and Karthik grew restless.

At his turn, Karthik asked the receptionist, "Do I have a parcel?" and then Karthik meekly surrendered by mumbling, "I am 505."

The name is dead. Long live the 'name'!

CHAPTER FOUR

The Mystical Maya Bazaar

Sh... 4:30 p.m. factory siren, finally! The nerve-wracking second day's training on Psycho-Cybernetics was coming to a close, with Consultant Dr Kanakapathy summarising the day's takeaway points.

The fifty trainees were all fresh engineering graduates appointed as Engineer Trainees (ET) at the behemoth of a public sector company, Bharat Power in Trichy, India (company). These ETs were recruited based on a very competitive pan-India recruitment process.

The Psycho-Cybernetics training was at the company's prestigious, cosy training room with the number 'F1.' In this company, in the 1980s, there were two of its kind (the other being F2) air-conditioned and fully curtained rooms. Aptly named F1, it was the ground zero from where many chequered career pursuits got flagged and raced off. While a lot got padlocked at the home company, some raved up to national and international circuits. Those stories are for another day!

"Don't drink milk. Eat it," was a clear takeaway from Dr. Kanakapathy for Ram Kumar! This was an off-line comment made by Dr. Kanakapathy on how to eat, particularly milk, to help our digestive system.

Before concluding, Dr. Kanakapathy said, "Today is your company's payday." Then he went on, "Are you aware of the impact Bharat Power employees' salaries make on the local market? It is to be seen to be believed. Enjoy, guys!"

Indiran, sitting next to Ram Kumar, murmured, "Ram, that is a gross understatement by one-fifth times if we talk about our Maya Bazaar. Isn't it?"

Ram understood what Indiran meant – Maya Bazaar is not just a 'seen' to be believed phenomenon – it is alluring to all the five senses!

But Ram wasn't aware that it would transcend beyond his five senses today.

All ETs were too eager to rush out to escape Cybernetics and to splurge their newfound stipend money.

While leaving F1, Ram heard a whisper, "Buddy, looks like they are sure to make us psychos," from among the herd ahead of Ram. Ram wasn't sure if it was Durairaju who would go on to become the ebullience-personified of the group in the years to come.

"Not like that appa, understanding psycho subjects can help us in our career and life," Sashidhar, who would go on to become the forever moderator-par-excellence, said in a pleading tone.

Meantime, as the 'sealed' door of the room opened, a tsunami of 'smell,' 'odour,' 'stink,' 'aroma,' whatever you want to call it, swept them aside.

Indiran yelled from behind, "Dai, this is from the Maya Bazaar, the payday market!" The payday market makes an appearance on the evening of the salary day of the company and vanishes the next day to reappear again on the next pay day. It happens on the annual bonus payment day too.

As ETs came out of Training Centre, they saw blue plastic sheets, the 'make-shift shops' being spread on the pavements by each seller, just outside of the Training Centre's barbed wire fence. On all other days, the pavements wore a deserted look barring a few trainees walking on them, occasionally.

Today, there were many people unloading bundles of goods and spreading their wares on the foot paths on either side of the road. There were vendor carts too. The company security and administration, with a beefed-up presence, was regulating them to bring some order.

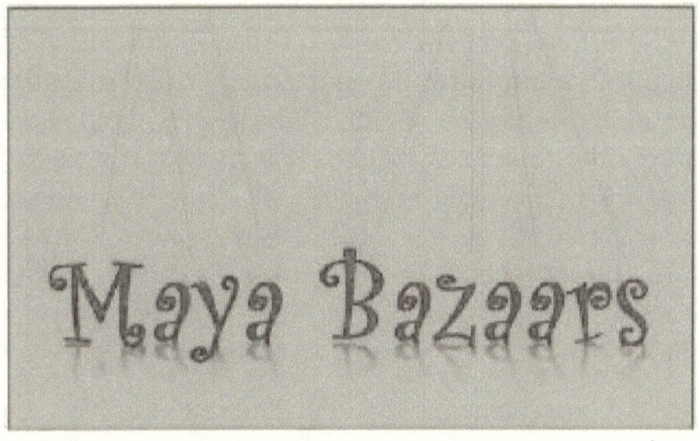

Indiran and Ram reached the dining hall of the Engineer's Trainee Hostel (ETH) for an early dinner.

The ETH was just 5 minutes' walk from the Training Centre. As they sat down at the stainless steel topped gleaming table, Indiran said, "I will keep my stomach half empty. We can eat at the Maya Bazaar some ethnic snacks."

Not to be outdone, E. Sarawan, sitting to the left of Indiran, said, "In that case, let me have my stomach only half full!" to complete the proverbial phrase, winking his right eye.

"Don't waste your winks. You may need more of it at the Maya Bazaar," Indiran teased in double meaning.

"Yes. You get to see Township gals all at one spot, the Maya Bazaar!" they said in chorus.

As Indiran and Ram prepared to step out, E. Sarawan and Nandhan joined them enthusiastically. As they walked out of ETH, Karnan and Sathish Babu, possibly the earliest pair formed in the batch, too joined them.

With each other's hands on their shoulders, they stepped out towards Maya Bazaar, symbolising the onset of a life-long bonhomie. But ahead of them, there were other groups of ETs heading towards the payday market. Danush and Murugavel broke away from one of the groups and were seen rushing ahead. Danush and Murugavel had the nicknames of Dax and Murux respectively, and both among their other endeavours and talents, were accomplished carrom players.

On all other nights, the Training Centre area would be desolated and dark, barring some streetlights at distances. Today, the area was buzzing with crowd, noise, and lights of varying sources - simple kerosene lanterns on carts of small-time vendors selling roasted peanuts, corn, pineapple, etc.; petromax lights for vendors of plastic and kitchen wares and battery-powered lights for bedsheet/garment merchants – symbolising the status of their segments of businesses.

Above all, the mix of aroma from sambrani, agarbathi, jack fruits and dried fish filled the air – it was not just inviting but enticing.

In short, it had that un-designed and organically evolved carnival vibe.

Nandhan wanted to buy a bedsheet at the garment outlet; he scanned through the lot, picked one, and asked Ram.

"Ram, is this good?"

Ram thought the vendor could have sourced bedsheets and towels from the nearby city of Karur.

Before Ram could answer, they overheard a voice from behind.

"Enna Nandha deal done?" It was Dhanarajan.

"Not yet, Dhanam," Nandhan said. Dhanarajan is affectionately called Dhanam by the batchmates.

Dhanarajan touched the top layer of the bedsheet, placing his thumb on top and four other fingers underneath it, and 'felt' it.

"How much he is asking for?"

Nandhan, getting closer to Dhanarajan's ears, whispered the price.

Dhanam, "That is a good price. You may ask for a few rupees less for your satisfaction. First, they don't have overheads. You will get things here at retail showrooms' cost price. In addition.."

Nandhan was in a hurry to settle the deal, so he paid for the bedsheet and collected it from the vendor.

Ram reminded, "Dhanam, you were about to tell something else."

Dhanam continued from where he left, "Yes. Let me tell you. These people are self-made entrepreneurs. Small size business owners, face challenges in life and business. Many come from villages near my place. I empathise with them a lot. They are business owners; but we are after all salaried persons. Aren't we?"

Dhanarajan, normally a quiet guy at the training session, was in full flow, putting forward his dhananomics!

He was from a village, Inamkulatur in Trichy district in Tamil Nadu. He understood how these small businesses work, their challenges and how it would mutually benefit if buyers supported them. He sounded as the brand ambassador of Maya Bazaar. Ram gave a rapt attention to Dhanam.

"Did you notice our Ramachandran, Sashidhar, Sekar and Swaminathan flocking together?" queried Indiran.

"Yes. But what are they buying, Sambrani?" asked Sathish noticing them stopping in front of shop selling perfumes and incenses. The seller had placed few raw particles of sambrani on a charred cup with embers. The sweet vanilla aroma of benzoin spread its fragrance, with the wind making the little area around the shop, serene, albeit a short while.

"Oh. They were buying packets of agarbathis and some Swami pictures," spotted Nandhan.

"They are very religious. They perform sandhyavandanam every day without fail!" wondered E. Sarawan, with a little quilt.

That was the last time the group saw E. Sarawan. While they were looking for some eat outs, E Sarawan had already left the group.

"Where is this E Sarawan gone?" Ram asked Karnan.

"I don't know," retorted Karnan.

Sarawan, E Sarawan, a prolific writer and a wordsmith, had started a monthly magazine for the batch of ETs called Impulse. Every month, he would prepare the material, get Impulse cyclostyled at the Training Centre, and circulate it. Prints and photocopies haven't arrived much in those days. Impulse, in many ways, had started making waves, and the batch was beginning to find common ground with it.

"Maybe, he smelt some juicy gossip around. Material for the next month's Impulse!" quipped Indiran.

"Tell me one thing da. Anyone asking him his name, he always adds his initial E to his name. Peculiar, isn't it?" Asked an intrigued Sathish.

"Forget that. Do you know his hometown, too, carries an initial? It is N. Paravur in Kerala," quipped Indiran, adding to the intrigue.

"Good, we escaped from the eyes of Impulse!" said Sathish, heaving a sign of relief. Sathish, as he took his stride, now freely fluttering his bell-bottom pants in an attempt to cause a few weak hearts around to flutter. Two Township girls passed by the group; did they giggle? Sathish was sure they did.

Indiran stopped at the next cart, where sliced totapuri mangoes sprinkled with a mix of country salt and chilli flakes were in the offering. Sathish ordered slices for the group and paid for them. Sathish had volunteered to keep the accounts, which he did meticulously. Later in the night, he would walk to all the group member's rooms with a coin/change box to collect monies and settle the accounts by that night itself, leaving no carry forwards. Sathish ensured that all settlement accounts were reconciled by the EOD – a perfect financial control practice.

Nandhan noticed that something was peculiar in the way Karnan picked the mango slice. He was picking the slice gently with the tips of his thumb and forefinger, in his left hand!

"Hi, Karna, why are you using your left hand for eating?" he asked knowing Karnan's natural hand was right.

"Nandha, here in Maya Bazaar, you don't have a chance to wash your hands with water after eating. In case of any emergency, like a dusty wind, your natural hand will rush to your eyes to rub. This can avoid such mishaps!" said Karnan. What a foresight! Small things make perfection, but perfection is no small thing!

The salty, sour-cum-chilli tinge, particularly from the chilli flakes on the mango slice, stayed on ones' tongues long, long after the piece had travelled deep into the stomach – no chance for the factory-made masala powder, the group believed.

E. Sarawan, of course, missed the slice and the tinge. Maybe he got hold of much juicier and spicier stuff, but who knows? But Ram was in a different mood, focusing on observations rather than talking.

The batch had several ETs from states other than Tamil Nadu. Some were from other southern states, a few from the Hindi belt and even from Odhisa. Hindi (or lack of Tamil knowledge) bonded them together, and they were called the Hindi gang by ETs from Tamil Nadu (a subtle, 'Tamil theriyathu poda' gang?). Satbir Singh and Sidhu Mohanty from this gang were trying to bargain for some plastic wares in their broken Tamil with a vendor. The ever-debonair Durairaju saw this and willingly stepped in. "Satbir, need help?"

Raju bargained and settled the deal for them; Raju started to become the darling of the gang!

Halwa stall was close by, with halwa heaps in display resembling the Trichy city's dark brown Rock Fort. Roving eyes of Raju spotted a senior batch ET, Sathyan, buying halwa.

"Hi Sidhu, note there, Sathyan is buying halwa!" Raju screamed with excitement.

"Raju, why are you so excited?" asked Sidhu.

"Sidhu, just watch him; he will next go to the flower stall and buy strands of jasmine! Tonight, they will have maja!" Raju almost screamed.

"What are you saying? What is maja?" an 'innocent' Sidhu asked.

Raju pulled Sidhu aside and tutored him on how the combo of halwa and jasmine play a key role in the marital life of couples, as per Tamil movies.

A wide-mouthed Sidhu listened to Raju with rapt attention - it took a while for him to close his mouth.

Meantime, there was some commotion few stalls away. A fit of rage, argument between two sellers who had spread their ware on the pavement and a security guard of the company was mediating between them.

Satbir, who could not understand Tamil, asked Raju, "What is the matter, Raju?"

"This is a border fight. These two sellers are accusing each other of encroachment on their areas on the pavement. Need a Line of Control here, too!" Raju said with some sarcasm.

The security guard yelled at the two sellers, "This Maya Bazaar show is going to last only for 7 to 8 hours tonight. In this, you are having a territorial fight!" The group skirted around the fight and moved on.

But the security guard's message kept lingering in Ram's mind.

The 'dreik,' 'dreik' sound at the next stall attracted the attention. It was peanuts getting roasted in hot sand. A deep pan over the stove was partly filled with sand. Peanuts dropped into it were allowed to get heated and roasted. The sound of 'dreik' was from the metallic skimmer put in stirring action by the vendor.

Sathish proposed, "Guys, let us have some peanuts," and ordered four packets. The vendor picked the hot peanuts with a smaller skimmer from the pan and shook it a little so that the last few sand particles dropped away. He then tore a page of an old Kumudham Tamil weekly magazine, rolled it up into a cone, and placed peanuts into it - before a head-tilted - Nandhan could do a quick reading of that Kumudham's page.

"You don't want to leave even that one page?" quipped Sathish at Nandhan. You guessed it correctly. Nandhan was a bookworm who enjoyed reading and, over time, would turn into a monstrous 'book-alligator.'

Each one collected a cone open at the top. The group's Paytm of those days, Sathish, as usual, paid for the peanuts.

After some more shopping and more eating, the group finally got to see E. Sarawan.

Ahead of the road, the group saw again those two Township girls, who had passed by them earlier. They are daughters of the company employees and were living near the C sector shopping centre. The two-some were quite well known in the Township, particularly to the Township lads, and can be found at any outings, gatherings in the Township.

And there, not far behind those girls, were Dax and Murux. Like in the game of carrom, one coin has to follow the red coin (aka queen) into the pocket; Dax and Murux were following these two queens. They were matching their pace with the gals, and oh, wait, were they talking to them, too? Wow, that was too fast-within a few months of joining the company!

E. Sarawan suddenly appeared at the scene from nowhere and pushed ahead and caught up with Dax and Murux. He had a chat with Dax and Murux and returned to the group with a smile.

"Red pocketed? Game over? Any scoop?" Sathish was shooting questions.

"No. Wait for the next Impulse," was the cryptic reply from a tight-lipped E. Sarawan.

The group knew a spicy story would go on print in the next month's Impulse.

But Ram was in a different world, ruminating, 'What can be more piquant than this mystical Maya Bazaar?'

It was getting close to midnight and the Maya Bazaar was slowly wearing down. The groups of ETs returned to their hostel rooms, with their thoughts on the following day's training.

Next morning as Ram walked towards Training Centre, along with other trainees, he glanced at the road. The stretch that was so lively last night, looked abandoned now. The company's administration had done a great job in collecting all trash and cleaning up the entire bazaar, overnight.

'Cleaned up, but lost life!' What an irony Ram imagined. His mind was wavering into some profound thoughts – he felt a little shiver in his body, too. Was it goosebumps?

The buzz, excitement, five senses-feeder, fun, interactions, fights, arguments, romances, the economic cycle of the bazaar, whatever there was, were all gone - they were so short-lived. But unmindful of all these ephemerals, this 'ruthless' enduring time moves on!

Was Ram seeing a message beyond the five senses?

The there-yesterday-gone-today phenomenon, the bazaar's transient nature, struck deep in his mind.

No wonder it is called the Maya Bazaar, he reckoned!

A little bit of mixed aroma of the Maya Bazaar was still in the air.

While entering Training Centre, Ram took a deep breath of the left-over aroma and settled down for the next round of Psycho-Cybernetics – in existential terms, to play his role in the mother of all maya bazaars called, life.

CHAPTER FIVE

The Unknown Man

Prem Kumar can never forget his first career-day. He clearly remembers that day even after more than three decades.

His long career may have over hundreds and thousands of eventful days, but his first career-day remains evergreen in his memory. This is purely due to an unknown man, for his very simple act of unsolicited kindness. Time flies, as they say, but some moments are frozen in it; this is one such rare fossil that Prem has treasured in his memory. This unknown man is his first-day hero.

It was in November 1979. Prem received an appointment letter from Bharat Power (company) for a Rs. 750 per month Engineer Trainee position. This was after he went through a pan-India recruitment process in which fifty engineers were selected.

After some enquiries with some knowledgeable people, he decided to join this colossal power-to-the-people company. The Tamil Nadu state transport bus service, then called Thiruvalluvar Transport Corporation, took him from Coimbatore to Trichy for a ticket fare of, which he still remembers, Rs. 10:30 for a 5-hour journey.

As advised in the appointment letter, Prem reported to the warden of the Engineers' Trainees Hostel (ETH), near the Training Centre of BHEL, on the Trichy – Thanjavur Road. The warden was Mr. Nagarathinam, an ex-serviceman. He allotted him a room in the hostel. Sporting a disarming smile, he did make great first impressions with his friendly disposition.

Some of the batch mates had joined the company a couple of weeks before. They have been through the procedures of joining and were ready with their guidance notes.

"Leave very early in the morning. You have to trek a long way to the Personnel department in building number 24, along the RPS road," said one.

"There is practically no private transport facility available."

RPS is the abbreviation for the rolled products store. Prem wasn't aware then that he would be facing a barrage of three letter abbreviations in the years to come. Apart from building number 24, there were numerous numbered buildings, none of them having their numbers displayed on their top!

"Is it possible to get a lift from the employees driving to their offices in two-wheelers?" he asked.

"Scores of two-wheelers would be passing by the road, but no one will help," was the warning.

So, Prem got ready early in the morning, rushed to get his first breakfast in the ETH mess, and started his first-ever step in his career.

Streams of two-wheelers, coveted Bajajs, budget Vijays and military-look-Lambrettas, doot-doot Rajdoots, stylish Yezdis, and poor peddle-pusher bicycles were all rushing, which later Prem came to know, to beat the time-punch-clocks.

Prem was hoping that at least one among the hundreds would stop and give him a lift to the Personnel department. He attempted to stop one of the motorists, he refused, the second one was worse; he didn't even give me a glance!

Prem was disgusted.

He thought: 'What kind of people these are?'

..'no compassion for a new recruit,'

..'no regard for a fellow human being seeking help!'

He was pondering, 'Have I taken the right decision in joining a company whose employees are a bunch of selfish people?'

..'why didn't this company arrange for transport for me?'

Prem decided not to ask for any more help and continued walking, wiping his sweat.

Then the miracle happened!

A bicyclist overtook Prem and stopped beside him, put his left foot down and asked Prem, "Would like to be dropped at the building number 24?"

Prem couldn't believe his ears!

Judging that it is going to be a long distance of peddle-pushing, Prem politely refused the offer. However, this good Samaritan insisted on helping and so, Prem sat on the carrier rack at the backside of the bicycle. It was an up-hill peddling for a good 20 minutes!

There were practically no buildings on both sides of the road. The terrain on either side had well-grown eucalyptus trees spread around. 'They must have been planted when the factory was set up,' Prem thought. Otherwise, the stretch was barren. Occasional dusty winds brushed past them.

In between the journey, it appeared that the good Samaritan was struggling to pedal. Prem offered to pedal, which he graciously refused.

Prem was gratefully applauding this person in his thoughts.

'What a great person is this guy. So empathetic! Coming out and helping me voluntarily! He is truly a blessed soul.'

After some 20 minutes, they reached the bicycle stand near the main gate of the company. The good Samaritan showed Prem building number 24 that was adjacent to the main gate and said, "I too work in this building."

Prem dismounted from the bicycle from the left side and profusely thanked him as he watched the good Samaritan get down. He put his left foot down and with a bit of a struggle brought down his right foot too.

After sporting a smile and bidding bye to Prem, he moved to park his bicycle inside the stand, in a movement that was jerky.

Prem was dumbfounded by what he saw; the person's right leg had a club foot disability!

CHAPTER SIX

A Storm in a Teacup!

"I can't wait until the cows come home," thundered Vinay Bhatia, Director of Projects at Apex Consulting Services (ACS). It was during the first quarter project status review meeting at the ACS headquarters in Mumbai. At the receiving end was a naïve Gopalakrishnan, the Graduate Trainee from the Project Management department. He wondered what cows have to do with project slippages.

Mr. Bhatia threw the project status report back to Gopal and said, "Better to bounce this off to Ajay to iron out the kinks before showing it to me tomorrow," and then dialled Ajay,

"Ajay, there is something falling between the cracks in this report from this new kid on the block. Want you to do the fine-combing. This greenhorn needs some sharpening."

Gopal's bewilderment hit the roof, as the terms 'greenhorn,' 'bouncing off,' 'ironing the kinks,' 'fine-combing' etc. were out of his language radar. Although these are proper words, Gopal could feel that they carried different meanings in this context and mumbled, "But, I always got good marks in English in school."

Gopal, from a village in south Tamil Nadu, had a simple upbringing. He graduated from an engineering college in a nearby small town, becoming the first-ever graduate in his family lineage.

Since joining ACS, he has been bamboozled with the barrage of clichés and idioms from Mr. Bhatia every day. He was already struggling to cope with the pace of Mumbai metro life. Gopal got closer to his colleague Ajay Kumar, a Delhiite, who doubled up as the 'translator' of Mr. Bhatia's clichés, idioms, and expressions. Ajay guided Gopal in fine-tuning the report.

The next day at 10:00 a.m., Gopal walked into Mr. Bhatia's cabin with the revised report and a little more confidence.

Glancing through the report, Mr. Bhatia said "Looks good, but needs more meat on the bone" making Gopal wonder why Mr. Bhatia is talking about food when it is not lunchtime yet.

Looking into the report, Bhatia continued unabated, "Want to squeeze this vendor? There is no use flogging a dead horse; we can't be chasing the tail." Closing the report, he ordered, "Get back to the drawing board and finish this report today, as we have to launch before the rubber hits the road." A perplexed Gopal had nowhere to run but to Ajay. Ajay helped Gopal decipher the boss's feedback and successfully finished the report.

Being a diligent learner, Gopal quickly settled in his project management role. He also spent time with Ajay to derive contextual meaning out of Bhatia's daily utterances, in addition to learning about clichés from the internet. By now, he had a fair understanding of the Bhatia-speak.

Gopal's enthusiasm gradually led to an overload of projects. A shrewd Mr. Bhatia sensed this quickly, and in the next weekly meeting, he said, "Gopal, I find your plate is full now; pass on your DCD project to Rajinder."

Pointing to Rajinder, he said, "Rajinder, you take over the project from today. Remember, the deadline is this year-end."

After the meeting, Gopal met Rajinder in his office. Rajinder cryptically said, "Leave the file on my desk. I will look into it." It appeared that Rajinder was not keen on taking over the project halfway through. Gopal duly sent a hand-over e-mail to Rajinder, copying Mr. Bhatia.

Year-end was approaching; daily follow-ups were the order of the day. Everyone was staying late and taking work home.

As the Head of Projects, Mr. Bhatia was the most worried, "Guys, I am running like a headless chicken. We should hit the bull's eye this year too." He was upset with some projects that were in red.

This Monday morning, as everyone was driving to the office, a text message from Mr. Bhatia hit their mobiles, 'Let us have a morning-shout at 9.' With all project managers assembled, it was a pure monologue, living up to its name, the morning 'shout.'

Project by project, Bhatia blasted managers on the left, right, and centre. "If we don't meet the deadline, there will be heavy penalties from the clients. Then heads will roll," he openly threatened. It was Gopal's baptism into the year-end frenzy, and he was relieved that all his projects were out of the red.

When the next item in the agenda, DCD project was discussed, Gopal was in for a shock. Mr. Bhatia yelled, "Gopal, your DCD project is in a royal mess. How are you going to bridge the gap?"

With the year-end stress upon him, Mr. Bhatia forgot about the change in the project ownership.

Gopal tried to explain, "Mr. Bhatia, you asked me to.."

"Stop it and come to the point. How are you going to deliver?" Bhatia raised his voice.

Gopal gathered courage, "Sir, but I have handed..."

Bhatia went wild, "No more stories! Can't wait for the other shoe to drop. Time is up for you. Keep it short and simple. In few words.. come on.., come on..," intimidatingly, he went on, on and on.

What Gopal said next stunned all, including Mr. Bhatia.

"Sir, what is the point in barking at the wrong tree!"

CHAPTER SEVEN

The Bald and the Beautiful

What do you think Jeff Bezos, Anupam Kher, Andre Agassi, Rajinikanth, and I have in common?

"Well done!" for those who got the 'bald' answer, and "Well tried!" for those who are still scratching their heads for being on the right spot!

Do you know about the newest classification of men: 'those who are bald' and 'those who want to be?'

Want to be? You may be surprised if you are one of those unfortunate 'Haves.' Being a 'Have-not,' I can explain why.

Philip Harrison, a senior research scientist, from the Genome Research Centre in Geneva, too was sceptical, initially, like you are. He is a changed man now and is happy to shed his hair!

A few months ago, I was at a social gathering with my colleague, Ravi Kumar. There, he introduced me to Dr, Philip Harrison.

"Tony, meet Dr. Harrison," Ravi introduced him to me.

My name is Thanikachalam Subramanian, for convenience sake known as, 'Tony.' I said, "Hai,

Dr. Harrison, nice meeting you. I am Tony," extending my hand.

Dr. Harrison shook my hand firmly as he looked at my top – and lingered at it far longer than the customary few seconds.

Nearly two decades of corporate life had reaped its rewards on my head-top. It had slowly gone barren.

I discovered his face with some difficulty, amidst a thick mane, to exchange a smile. He had his hair all over the face, a thick salt-pepper beard and the only parts that were visible were his little forehead, eyeballs, nose, and mouth, when he chose to open it.

I have not seen a more perfect match between the name and the looks of a person than Dr. Harrison. The sight of his hairy face made me feel allergic to him.

However, eager to know the details of his genome research, I asked him what he is up to, without realising that the conversation that followed is going to change the course of Dr. Harrison's $1.6 billion genome research project.

"Tony," Dr, Harrison said with a grin, "in short, my research is going to solve your problem," while he glanced, yet again, at my 'perfect' head.

"My problem? I do not seem to have a problem," I said with a queer in my voice.

He reluctantly said, "You see, you have been losing your hair and ..."

I immediately interjected, "I am sorry, Dr. Harrison, I am not losing anything. In fact, I thought

I was gaining more face," to give him a lesson on the power of positive thinking.

"Please allow me to explain about this research," he pleaded. Then he explained how he and his team are tracing the gene code that is the root cause of MPB (Male Pattern Baldness), i.e., hair-loss in men, and that one-day they will come up with a breakthrough solution that will eliminate the hair-loss problem, and men forever will be saved from baldness.

"No," I screamed, "Dr. Harrison, I am sorry to say that your research is terribly misdirected. Your research should be the other way around. You should identify the root cause for hair growth and eliminate it."

Then I explained to him the virtues of having a perfect head. I told him there are more to baldies than it meets the eye; they are wiser, level-headed and are good managers and achievers.

"In fact, Dr. Harrison, bald men are considered sexier," I told him with a twinkle in my eyes. I could see the spark in his eyes, but I wasn't sure if he was fully convinced. "Philip, are you still not convinced?" I used his first name for the first time.

Then I told him I have evidence from Anthropology, Business Management and Health Sciences to prove my point that men today are indeed dying to become bald.

He said half-heartedly, "Please go ahead."

I explained to him about the theory of evolution of Homo sapiens.

"Philip, what does theory of evolution teach us on the hairy issue?" I asked and paused and said, "The more the hair you have, the more you are akin to the monkey, my dear Philip!"

Then I said to myself, 'Do not loss your heart Philip, just the hair, and I will show how you can climb up the ladder of evolution.'

"That is interesting," said Philip, "What about other evidences," for the first time he showed a little excitement.

"Philip, do you agree that time is the most precious resource available to human being?" I asked.

Philip agreed and said, "Yes, indeed, Tony, every minute is valuable in life."

That is the opening I waited for and duly gate-crashed, "Philip, the amount of time that 'Have-nots' save is unbelievable. They save 9 minutes per shower and hair drying, 10 minutes per mirror-view and hair adjustment, 60 minutes per hair-dye cycle, 12 minutes per hair-cut cycle, to mention a few," and "In all, a whopping 350 hours saved per year! And 10,500 hours during their entire bald-years life!" I said without gasping.

Philip went speechless and now appeared to get a bit jealous about the virtues of being a 'Have-not.'

"What about further support from Health Sciences?" mumbled Philip.

I roared, "Philip, being bald means being more hygienic. I will tell you why," and I said, "You will agree that ability to think is the one factor that distinguishes human from animals."

"Yeah," he readily agreed.

I further explained the two vital physical activities that thinking involves, i.e., 'scratching the head' and 'biting nails!'

Of course, no need to mention what hair means in hygiene parlance - one has only to recall the last time when s/he unearthed a strand of hair from her/his dinner plate.

"Philip," drawing his attention, I said, "Now let us get deeper into the process of thinking. Imagine the 'Haves' digging their nails into their hairy top, like a shovel digging the ground at a construction site, and ending up scooping zillions of microbes in their nail tips."

I could sense Philip has started shivering and I continued unabated, "Philip, let us get into the filthiest stage of the thinking process, of putting your nails between your teeth, chewing it and finally biting it!"

That was the last nail on Philip's head, and he left the gathering in a hurry.

I followed him, yelling, "Philip, where are you going?"

Philip looked back as he rushed towards his car saying, "Tony, I am rushing. I've two critical things to do immediately. A project course correction and an appointment with my barber!"

A week later, the $1.6 billion genome research project took a 'U' turn for the benefit of **man**kind, and Philip regained his face.

CHAPTER EIGHT

The 'Luscious' Dining Table

The Appetiser

The so-called 'Azpire Apparels obscene logo controversy' stunned me as well as confused me.

I came to know of it from Murthy, who I bumped into at the Chennai domestic air terminal, a few months ago.

It was a coincidental meeting - we were both waiting for our flights - his to Bengaluru and mine to Coimbatore. My flight was about an hour later than his.

"Obscene logo? Which one?" I asked Murthy curiously.

Murthy opened his smartphone and showed me the logo while saying, "An activist raised a complaint with the police that this logo is insulting and offensive towards women. What do you think?"

"Murthy, I have seen this logo of this company, Azpire Apparels, before. It didn't occur to me as obscene then. But now, after you mentioned the controversy, the overlapping arrangement of letters A & A does appear like a woman spreading her legs, and the overlapping pattern highlights the ...I mean, the private part...oh my God!" I squirmed.

Murthy went on, "You know, these ad agencies rake big sums for such logos and campaigns." Murthy should know better. He has an MBA with a marketing specialisation from IIM Calcutta and works for a marketing agency in Bengaluru.

Looking at the logo again, something 'rang a bell' in my mind, and I was dead sure.

"Murthy, forget about the offensiveness of the logo. In the first place, this logo is not original. It is plagiarised!" I thundered.

Taken aback by my assertions, Murthy countered in disbelief, "How do you say that?"

"Decades ago, I witnessed this logo evolve in our company at Raju's desk," I said.

"You mean Bharat.." said Murthy with a smirk.

"No. No. I didn't mean that... but a team member at our lunch table drew this," I said with firmness.

Meantime, the devil in my mind was taking a trip down that dirty memory lane. It was during our team lunch sessions Raju, our group's XXX matter guru, would conduct impromptu tutorials on XXX topics, at times illustrating different intercourse postures with livid sketches.

'Where have all those masterpieces gone?' 'Those were collectors' items'; my devil was still on a deep, stinky, nostalgic trip.

Murthy's next question woke me up.

"So, were you guys doing creative stuff too?" Muthu asked in utter wonderment. Murthy left our company long ago to pursue his MBA.

Sitting in a public place, considering decency and decorum, I was hesitant to explain the details of our s-exploits at Raju's desk during lunchtime, and I earnestly wished to change the topic.

Hence, I gave a long pause.

Sensing my hesitation, Murthy nudged, "Come on da, tell me about the logo design."

"Murthy, it has been decades. True. Something like the logo evolved at our lunch table." I was trying to be curt and, in a hurry, close this 'dirty' subject.

Murthy may have sniffed that there is some filthy inside story and insisted, "I need to know the full story. About all the team members and how the logo evolved. Please da."

'Is Murthy probing too much?' His insistence gave me a suspicion that Murthy had some axe to grind against the ad agency.

'Who knows?'

Meantime, there was an announcement that the flight to Bengaluru would be delayed by an hour.

Murthy jumped and went on, "See, my flight is delayed. We have all the time. Tell me the story in detail. Did Raju design the logo? About each team member! All, all the details!"

Murthy continued to plead, "You see, I left the company too early, don't know much about many guys," Murthy tried to strike the emotive card.

I quickly retorted, "But Murthy, you didn't leave. You jumped the employment bond and absconded...." I thought this needling would alter the course of our conversation.

But Murthy was a step ahead. Brushing aside my provocation, he tried to placate me, "And you claim to be a storyteller, too. Go ahead and spill the beans, man."

Murthy was unstoppable and was using all the tricks from the copybook of a proud MBA from a premier institute.

Unable to resist anymore, I started to narrate this story, in full, to prove two things: establish beyond doubt the owner of coveted logo and spot the black sheep who passed on the logo design to the ad agency.

The story begins with the first abode of the lunch gang, my own department.

Getting Kicked Out!

"**W**as that too much of a mess?" I was bewildered.

We were in our early years in the company. Along with my fellow Engineer Trainee batchmates, I was lunching at my desk in my office at my department called Industrial Engineering.

Just moments ago, my fuming, well-built juggernaut of a boss, pointing to me, was telling Rayappa, "Rayappa, move his desk here, today," as he showed a place right in front of his cabin door, with an authoritative emphasis on 'today.'

He obviously wanted my desk and me to be placed under close watch. But why?

The root cause, it appears, was the boisterous bonhomie that we, the batchmates, used to have every day at the lunch table at my desk in our department.

Rayappa, a celibate, well-known amongst our batchmates, was our all-in-all Office Adm. He duly nodded his head to the big boss, albeit gently - not to disturb the setting he had painstakingly done with the last few hair strands to cover his bald head.

Rayappa had by then mastered the art of nodding. My own receding headline compelled me not to take my eyes off such awkward moments and more importantly, remedies that come by.

Not to invite further trouble, we decided to ditch my department and migrate to a department called Field Engineering & Services (FES) as our next stop for our lunch gathering.

Alas, the future corporate leaders were literally shown the door just for a 'chat.' No enquiry, no deliberation, but the judgement was delivered!

When I completed narrating this part, an amused Murthy asked, "So, you guys were kicked out! But did FES welcome you?" The story there on gets more intriguing.

Feeling Easy & Safe

In the days, months, and years to come, FES bore the brunt of us. But that did not come as a surprise, as FES was already notorious for being the 'last resort' to company-rebels.

The lunch brigade was primarily a group of Engineer Trainees of my batch and the like-minded whose offices were in the mysteriously, non-sequentially, twin numbered, 2&4 building.

But where is the missing number 3? True to his puzzle proficiency, Sarwan joined the gang to fill in the missing number of building number 3, the Central Laboratory of the company.

Others included Karna, the host Raju and me. The table became so notorious and inviting that some more members joined us whenever they weren't on official tours. They are Satvinder Singh, Amar Singh (of another batch) and the ever-ebullient Jainath

Kumar (our senior). They, too, added more flavour and decibels to our already outrageously spicy 'chat.'

The environment at FES, for us, the adolescents, meant that lunch was more than food for the stomach.

Raju, in the prime of his form, dished out extra-large portions of luscious mouth-watering 'side dishes.' Hold on. More about it later!

Needless to say, we were more than hungry for lunchtime, not the lunch per se.

But please wait. Murthy had insisted on an update on every team member, as he left the company too early and missed all the fun, you see. Forgive me if this is becoming a cliché.

Therefore, we will head to the lunch table after brief intros of key team members and bringing them, one by one, on the table.

The Scratch & Win Champion

Sarwan, the newly minted metallurgist from IIT Madras, was surely a treasured specimen of the company's Central Laboratory. His frail structure was held together by the company's sturdy grey uniform and of course the tight belt at his hip. He would be engaged in scratching failure specimens and ogling them under an electron microscope to figure out disorders in microstructures, with the glee of a peeping tom.

In these haphazard structures he would witness rangoli spectacles. His occasional 'eureka' would reverberate through the building, even causing few cracks on Lab walls. More importantly, they echoed at the corridors of power.

This raw ore turned the bruises that he received into polishing strokes and ended as a precious jewel in the crown. He had the wherewithal to literally scratch his way to glory!

At the stroke of lunchtime, as waves of employees stormed dirt cheap, subsidised canteens, this wafer-thin specimen would get swept aside 2&4 building shores as collateral damage.

To get rejuvenated at the altar!

The Enslaved

'You can't manage what you can't measure' was the mantra of my function, Industrial Engineering.

To be brute, this was already a tall order, in the company. However, this function had the ambition to offer strategy consultancy beyond the shores, now to the employees' coop bank (ECB)!

As a budding specialist on measurement, I visited the ECB's Head Office in A sector of the company's Township and their branch in building number 24. I sat inside their caged counters, 'studying' the work of bank staff. It was a nice feeling to know that you are being paid to watch others work.

We gave numerous recommendations that would enable the bank to turn the corner; the last I heard was that they did turn a couple of corners to get their HO relocated to the B sector of the Township!

Come 12:30 pm, I would unleash myself from captivity and rush to FES to join fellow gangsters.

Freedom at mid-day!

The Monk Who Pushed Trolleys

Karna yearned to be a part of a direct value-adding function and headed towards the production department. His production bay manufactured headers, a key component of the power plant's boiler system. With strong fundamentals, he would produce detailed plans with great mindfulness, dreaming of perfect execution. All in vain! Each time, his never-say-fine boss would deliberately find a hole in the blueprint to puncture his dreams, turning them into nightmares.

Karna, the man of action, would orchestrate not just all the Ms needed for production shops to achieve targeted tonnages but beyond. With the lines of responsibilities blurring at the borders of the production shop floor bays, it was left to engineers like Karna at the shop floors to push the trolleys with WIP (work-in-progress) into the next bay in the production line – a job of the unskilled, elsewhere.

Come what may, at lunchtime, wiping his sweat, the monk who pushed trolleys would steam in for lunch at FES – to get recharged.

The Master and the Honeytrap

As soon as adequate quorum got reached at his desk, Raju would pull out an A0 size drawing printout and spread it over his table, ensuring that the plain backside comes on top. We thought it was a good idea to dine on a clean sheet - but we didn't realise its multi-purpose utility, initially.

"Raju, make sure this drawing is not required for your job," one of us would warn Raju, knowing how mischievously careless he could be.

Raju would casually reply, "Ahre, never mind. This is going to be useful now as a lunch table-spread! Be satisfied, buddy."

We would pick our respective tiffin boxes and unpack one container at a time. Before one could see what dish he has got, each one would start peeping at others' containers! Alas, all human sensory organs are still wired to this peeping - may be the evolution is still a work-in-progress.

The next step is to exchange/share the dishes, aka 'pouncing' and 'poaching,' which is another evolutionary WIP!

In the meantime, someone more cultured like Satvindar would attempt to establish some table manners, but in vain.

Among all the dishes, tomato curry would be a major attraction for non-culinary reasons. On top of his voice, Raju would say, "Oh! Menses curry ah?"

We were taken aback by the comment, initially. Many of us would wriggle at the mention and would keep away from tomato dishes for days.

Cool as a cucumber, Raju would munch the curry and say, "Yummy da. Just eat it," and launch his 'tutorials.'

By then, Raju was married already, many of us were still bachelors, and Sarwan was about to get married and was the keenest listener of Raju' lectures.'

After a few days of normalisation, we quietly reverted to tomato dishes. How can one keep away from the ubiquitous tomatoes, for too long?

A lack of whiteboards or PPT would not deter Raju. To demonstrate the 'points' and 'angles,' he would pick his pen and draw on the 'table-spread' using appropriate colours - the plain sheet as table-spread makes sense now, isn't it?

The discussions would be camouflaged with a liberal sprinkling of boiler terms like, 'pre heat,' 'super heat,' 'injector,' 'blowdown,' to deceive any overhearing outsider.

Occasionally, we used to have guest appearances from colleagues from the Chennai unit (on official duty to the parent unit in Trichy), shortly known as the DATA (Dearness Allowance and Travel Allowance) collection mission. They, too, would get sucked into the chat. That is when the staunch traditionalist Chandra Mohan threw more light on the 'broad daylight' advantage with the traditional *madisar* saree.

The honeytrap was irresistible!

Incidentally, the logo, now pirated, was just a part of a masterpiece at elementary / Level 1 of Raju's discourse!

We all listened to Raju with rapt attention as we munched our food. Sarwan, the JEE victor, who knows the value of preparation in cracking any 'entrance' test, was itching to peek into such a masterpiece of a specimen under the electron microscope to fathom further deep into the climax.

"We also made power plant boilers," I winked at Murthy, who was quietly listening all the while. A captivated Murthy may have surely thought, 'Did I jump the gun too soon?' about missed early learning opportunities.

The Climax

Back into his inquisitive mood, Murthy declared, "It is clear now that Raju is the rightful owner of the intellectual property right for the logo. I am certain it was plagiarised by the agency. But by any chance, did Raju sell the logo to them?"

I said, "I don't think Raju would have sold it. You know he is loud-mouthed. If he made a bounty selling this, he would have trumpeted it to the whole world!"

Murthy nodded and probed further, "Then someone else from the team would have passed on the logo to the ad agency. Tell me who could be that culprit."

I explained, "I am also a part of the team. Isn't that a conflict of interest for me to tell?"

Murthy comforted me, "Never mind. I trust your judgement. Go ahead."

After a brief pause, I made my call.

"Murthy, cutting a long story short, here is my take. Everyone initially didn't believe this theory. Later, one by one, they all started agreeing to this. Now, I, too, believe in this theory."

"Which theory?" Murthy asked with eagerness and restlessness.

I replied, "The Lab-Leak Theory."

Alone in a Crowd

I will not forget forever, for the wrong reasons, the day I landed in Dubai to take up a job in a bank. It was many decades ago.

At the outset, I was very pleased to see a representative from the bank holding a welcoming placard with my name 'Sampath Kumar' on it.

As I approached him, he extended his hand to say,

"Welcome to Dubai" and went on, "Aap..@*2#..&^@*.heh.."

My God! He was speaking to me in Hindi! I could make out only the occasional Aaps, Jee's, Wallas and Hehs! When I said that I could not speak Hindi, I could see the bewilderment on his face, which, till today, I encounter on the faces of everyday people whom I meet and 'speak' to.

Within the first few days of my arrival, I realised that apart from my fellow countrymen who are found everywhere in Dubai, the Iranians in grocery shops, Pakistani taxi drivers, Yemeni merchants, Arab colleagues et al were all trying to pick up a conversation with me in Hindi, knowing that I am an Indian! It dawned on me that knowledge of Hindi is very valuable in Dubai! I, the Hindi illiterate, really had a cultural shock of sorts!

Come on, I only thought I was at a safe light-year's distance away from the Hindi belt! How could I, a homegrown Tamilian, accept this Hindi imposition in a foreign land? I felt I was unfairly hit below the (Hindi) belt!

Even my son, Ajit, has not been left out and has been forced to learn Hindi as a second language under the Indian educational curriculum that is followed in his school. Ajit's spoken Tamil learning comes only from indirect means, from conversations at home and outside when we meet our Tamil friends, and from watching the Tamil TV channels. A formal Tamil language course is not available here, and my wife and I have so far resisted our temptations to teach him proper Tamil, considering the enormous language load already on him in learning English, Hindi and above all, the right-to-left Arabic!

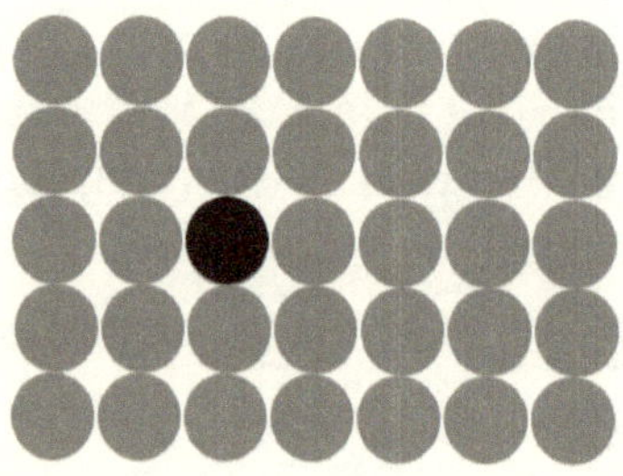

Our bank announced that the annual staff party would be held next Saturday. It is to be an outdoor event, a desert safari for staff and their family members. We were asked to assemble at the bank premises by 3 p.m. on that day.

On Saturday, along with my wife and my son Ajit, I drove in our Nissan Sunny car to our bank and parked the car at the usual parking area.

Around the area, I could see many white Toyota Land Cruisers sporting the signage 'Arabian Adventures' on their sides. Arabian Adventures is the tour operator engaged for this desert safari. They are expected to take us in these 4-wheel drives into the desert. A convoy of 11 such vehicles would take all of us together to the campsite in the interior desert.

We boarded the Land Cruiser number 5 along with a family of four of my friend and colleague Nilesh Sharma. The driver with sturdy features, I guessed, could be a Pathan or an Afghani. Ajit, my wife Nilesh, and his family members got into the back seats, and I took the front seat and closed the door. The driver, noting that I am an Indian, said something in Hindi. I squirmed.

Ajit saw my discomfort and translated what the driver said.

"Dad, he is asking you to close the door firmly."

Ajit by now has picked some Hindi from school, particularly spoken Hindi from his North Indian classmates. Ajit has got used to this routine of translating Hindi to me.

I closed the door firmly while looking at people in the back seats. I didn't miss the grin on Nilesh's face. Nilesh, the Mumbaiwala, knows my predicaments with Hindi.

Upon reaching the outskirts of Dubai, the Land Cruiser cruised at 130 - 140 kph on the well-laid highway, which had a speed limit of 120 kph. At times, the driver slowed down to 120 kph, to avoid the radar captures. These professional drivers know where the radars are positioned. But Dubai police too is trying to outsmart them with some surprise-mobile-radars and technologically advanced radars.

Both sides of the road were adorned by the vast oceans of sand and sand dunes. Soon we reached a collection point, where all the Land Cruisers arrived one by one. We were told that from that point we would enter into the desert. The drivers started deflating the car tyres to a great extent. This is to ensure stability of the vehicle while driving on the loose sand. Otherwise, the wheels would sink in the desert sand.

Before entering the desert, the driver said something in Hindi, and Nilesh duly translated it for me.

"Sampath, he is saying that we will be doing dune-bashing now. It is like a roller coaster on the sand. Anyone not comfortable with that can skip dune-bashing and can board the minibus stationed nearby, which will take them directly to the campsite."

I looked back to thank Nilesh, and I sensed that it was Ajit's turn to grin.

By the way, all of us in our Land Cruiser were ready for dune-bashing. The convoy was split into groups, with the navigators positioned on the lead 4W, and we set out to do dune-bashing.

We had a 'steady' bumpy ride for a while, and suddenly, the desert appeared to take the shape of a mountain range, a mountain of sand, loose sand.

Our 4W-drive tried to negotiate the contour of the terrain as it steadily climbed up the hill. The ground was slipping all the time under the tyres, and the 4W drive was tumbling every moment. I was already getting scared, and the sight to my left frightened me further, and I closed my eyes. I saw one of the 4Ws atop the sand hill, waited for a while and nose-dived at almost an angle perpendicular to Earth. When I opened my eyes, we too were descending at a great speed and landed at the valley, the Silicon Valley!

After reckless dune-bashing for some more time, we reached the top of another sand hill and thank God, we stepped out for a photo session.

It was nature in its purest form, the sand dunes sporting corduroy stripes running across endlessly, around 360 degrees, gave me a feeling of infinity. To me they looked like the fingerprints of wind and time on sand. The sight of the Sun setting on the ocean of sand was bewitching!

The colours of the twilight Sun and sky matching the shades of the sand dunes made a perfect designer statement, unmatched by any of man's creations. A humbling moment for the man!

As we arrived at the campsite, the Sun had set, and it was pitch dark outside, and the campsite was only spotlit. The site looked like the huge Martian crater where the Beagle two lost contact with Earth station. A circular deep pit of the size of a football ground, with lots of tents erected around the circumference. At the centre was a tripod-like structure for bonfire and there was a big rectangular arena for games and importantly, belly dancing!

There were many attractions around the camp for one to choose from.

Ladies were attracted towards henna artists. My wife Priya joined her lady-friends and they all moved toward the henna tent.

Sand skiing was another unique attraction. You climb up a sand hill and then using a sandboard ski down the hill, similar to skiing on snow.

Some Yemeni Bedouins had brought their camels to the site. The camel ride in the desert was available for a price.

"How much for a ride?" I asked the Bedouin.

"Pandrah @*& pachchees %^# Rupiah," he said.

Indian rupee has been the currency used in Dubai and other emirates for ages. Seven such emirates, including Dubai, joined together and formed the United Arab Emirates in 1971. UAE introduced Dirhams as their own currency. In spite of that, there is still a habit among many to call Dirhams as Rupiah!

I could make out that the camel keeper was mentioning numbers in Hindi and also Rupiah. But I was confused on why he is stating two numbers.

Before I could look around for a translation, both Nilesh and Ajit answered in tandem,

"Fifteen Dirhams for a single person. Twenty-five for two persons."

I paid twenty-five Dirhams for Ajit and I to take trip on the camel. I gathered courage to climb on a camel. Initially I thought that only the climbing was a huge challenge. I was wrong! In fact, every stage of the trip was a nightmare, be it climbing, taking a trip and the dismounting was all awkward!

"What a clumsy animal the camel is!" I yelled as Ajit and I got down.

Afterwards, Ajit joined the other boys and went up the sand hill for sand skiing.

I looked around for my friends and joined a group. It was predominantly an Indian crowd, along with some Pakistanis. As always, in such crowds, the topics for discussion hovered around cricket, Bollywood, politics, etc.

Initially, the conversations were in English. As time passed, certain situations arose for down-to-earth slang in Hindi. Slowly, the conversations, in full, jumped into Hindi. I could not continue and looked around for non-Indian groups. I could see Ajit was still busy sand skiing. I found a group of Arabs and Britishers and joined them.

Then there was an announcement for the start of party games. I located Ajit and my wife Priya and called back.

As Ajit joined me, he asked me, "I saw you from the sand hill. You were moving out from your group and going somewhere and joined another group."

"Yeah. I left the Hindi crowd to join the group that speaks English, the world language," I tried to rationalise.

After the party games, our CEO, an Arab, gave away staff awards and made a casual speech in English. He began his speech by welcoming the gathering in different languages, 'ahlan wa sahlan,' in Arabic, then 'welcome' in English, and then 'swagat' in Hindi, and so on. As we moved for dinner, a bonfire was lit near the rectangular spot. With a big bang, there appeared a spotlight on the arena and there was the belly dancer!

With our dinner plates, we rushed to assemble around the 'rectangular' ring. To a slow Arabic music at a low volume 'she' the slim Arab beauty, as thin as a wafer, started twisting her arms and belly slowly. The next number was in Hindi, and was faster, and her wriggle too was in rhythm with the tune. As the scale of the music varied, so did the twist of her muscles.

It was close to midnight. With the ending of the belly dancing, the event also came to a close.

The same Land Cruisers dropped us back at the bank. We bid bye to Nilesh and all our friends and wanted to rush back home as we were dead tired and were feeling so sleepy.

Ajit and my wife sat in the back seat of our Nissan Sunny. To keep me awake while driving, I tuned in to the local Tamil FM.

On air was this Tamil *Pattimandram* (a literary debate). In fact, they were re-running the debate that took place in Dubai last month.

A speaker was thundering, "Tamil is the oldest language, came into being even before stones, rocks, and sand... will one day become not only the Indian national language but the world language! And a day will come when all Americans and Europeans will line up to learn Tamil.." to the wildest applause from the audience.

We reached home and hit the bed at the soonest. As we lay in the bed, I could sense Ajit was feeling restless.

I asked him, "Hi Ajit, are you okay?"

In his half-sleep, Ajit muttered, "Appa... will you teach me Tamil starting tomorrow?"

I was too pleased to hear this, and my late-night-eyes brightened when I asked,

"I will, my dear, but why?"

Ajit mumbled, "When Tamil becomes the world language...."

"What if Tamil becomes a world language?" I asked him, thinking about the debate on Tamil FM on our drive back home.

Ajit continued, "Like you were in the party today, I do not to want appear clumsy!"

www.ingramcontent.com/pod-product-compliance
Lightning Source LLC
Chambersburg PA
CBHW031130160726
47989CB00017B/2757